Text copyright © Sam Williams 2006
Illustrations copyright © Mique Moriuchi 2006

First published in the United Kingdom in 2006
by Hodder Children's Books, a division of Hodder Headline Limited
338 Euston Road, London NW1 3BH
First published in the United States of America by Holiday House, Inc. in 2006
All Rights Reserved
Manufactured in China
www.holidayhouse.com
1 3 5 7 9 10 8 6 4 2

Library of Congress Cataloging-in-Publication Data
Williams, Sam, 1955-
    That's love / by Sam Williams ; illustrated by Mique Moriuchi. — 1st ed.
        p. cm.
    Summary: Illustrations and simple rhyming text describe
the subtle feelings that are love.
    ISBN-13: 978-0-8234-2028-5 (hardcover)
    ISBN-10: 0-8234-2028-0 (hardcover)
    [1. Love—fiction. 2. Stories in rhyme.]
I. Moriuchi, Mique, ill. II. Title.
    PZ8.3.W679266Tha 2006
    [E]— dc22
    2005035753

For Linda, Sam, Helen, and William (S.W.)   For Aki, Papa, Dan, Rich, Otti & Dave Onion (M.M.)

That's Love

by Sam Williams

illustrated by Mique Moriuchi

Holiday House / New York

I can name the leaves
and even the trees,
describe what I see
in the clouds on the breeze.

I can feel the air and taste the sea,

hear the BUZZ, BUZZ, BUZZ of a bumblebee.

Paint a color,

smell a flower,

draw a shape,

and name the hour.

Cross the ocean, whistle a tune,

make daisy chains, and fly to the moon.

I know ALL the countries of the world

(well, at least three).

And I can count to a million
and sing do-re-mi.

But I can't name the look
that I see on your face.

It isn't a color,
it isn't a place.

It's a feeling I feel,
so appealing,
so real.

Is it love?

The muddles,

the cuddles,

the laughs,

that's love.

A great big smile,
the softness of silence,

and all the while,
that's love.

Being kissed,

being missed,
that's love.

Wanting to share,

wanting to care,
that's love.

Knowing life is for living,

being forgiving
when it all goes wrong,
that's love.

Holding me when I cry,

helping me
to try
again,

that's love.

Seeing the good,
the way we all should.
Being special,
being there,
the way you are,
the way you care,

that's love.